Edwin John Ellis, William Blake

Facsimile of the Original OutlinesBefore Colouring

Of The Songs of Innocence and of Experience

Edwin John Ellis, William Blake

Facsimile of the Original OutlinesBefore Colouring
Of The Songs of Innocence and of Experience

ISBN/EAN: 9783744768160

Printed in Europe, USA, Canada, Australia, Japan

Cover: Foto ©Andreas Hilbeck / pixelio.de

More available books at **www.hansebooks.com**

FACSIMILE

OF THE

ORIGINAL OUTLINES BEFORE COLOURING

OF

The Songs

OF

Innocence and of Experience

EXECUTED BY

WILLIAM BLAKE

WITH AN INTRODUCTION

By EDWIN J. ELLIS

Author of " Fate in Arcadia " ; " Seen in Three Days " ; " Sancan the Bard "
and Co-Editor with W. B. Yeats of Blake's Works

LONDON

BERNARD QUARITCH, 15 PICCADILLY, W

1893

CONTENTS.

iv

INTRODUCTION.

FROM first to last there is a prevailing note of kindliness and affection about the Songs of Innocence and Experience which enables every reader to find companionship in them. Here we do not seek for profound phrases but for rest of heart, and for sweet musical sounds that shall make this rest a delight and an exaltation, so that we may not only enjoy, but be proud to enjoy such height with such peace. From time to time a mysterious allusion or a stern saying shocks our tranquility. Why did the man who wrote the beautiful Cradle Song, place it in the same volume with—

> "Thou mother of my mortal part,
> In cruelty didst frame my heart,
> And with false, self-deceiving tears
> Didst bind my nostrils, eyes, and ears."

And, "Who is Tirzah?" we ask ourselves, as we see the unexpected name at the head of the verses where these lines occur. We turn the pages again and soon find that all is not smooth and facile. The "Human Abstract" is not a soothing song, nor is the "Divine Image." Even the "Little Black Boy" is no nursery rhyme. The words of the Bard to Earth, and Earth's Answer, are weighty with some intention that does not at first appear.

These are not the only places where strange words bring us to a pause. Even the simplest of the rhymes has a puzzling counterpart on some other page under a similar title. We begin to feel that unless we know what the poet meant by this volume, and why he called Innocence and Experience rather than Innocence and Guilt the Two Contrary States of the Human Soul, we know nothing of his meaning and we are not reading our author at all, but playing with him, and perhaps deceiving ourselves.

In truth there is no book of Blake's so difficult to thoroughly understand as this collection of songs. The difficulty is increased by the sweetness and charm of the poetry. It seems almost a sin, and surely a folly, to awake ourselves with an effort of will from the half-dreamy enjoyment which we can receive here at our ease, and begin the serious task of giving ourselves an exact account of every word. The Introduction says that the Songs are addressed to children. To look deeply into them would be anything but a proof of profundity in the critic. They were intended to be enjoyed simply, so let us simply enjoy them.

This is the mood in which they have been received for half a century and more. An attempt to show what these Songs really contain arouses something akin to resentment. If there be, unfortunately, any symbolic purpose in them, such as destroyed all the later writings of the same author and made him pass for a madman in the end, then the less we hear of this melancholy blemish, and the sooner we are allowed to forget it, the better.

Those whose feelings are expressed in some such words as these always utter their view with an emphasis and a determination which shows that any attempt to differ from them would produce only anger, and would lead to no change in the attitude of their minds. And yet they are people with whom it is impossible not to sympathize. Their error and their anger spring from a true love of poetry, a love that is jealous of the entrance of symbolism into verse, as though this were an intrusion. The tricks of the writers of acrostics appear only less hateful to them. Symbolism, as they know, often springs from a systematic use of metaphor, persisted in until figures of speech become technical terms, so that what was once a beautiful image and a vivid illustration descends into a slavery of repetition and becomes—or would become but for its beauty—little better than an addition to that degraded language of the illiterate classes called slang. Symbolism is, indeed, all this, and more. But it is not necessarily prosaic. Eastern writers, as every reader of the Bible knows, are most poetic when most symbolic. Western minds grasp readily at Eastern symbols and, as the Puritans have proved too well, can almost force us to believe that, on modern lips, prose and symbolism are invariably found together. But for Edmund Spenser, Blake would be the only great modern Western symbolic poet. As it is, his richness of invention and significance of myth place him so far above and beyond Spenser that his writings practically begin and end the literature in which they must be classed.

No general account, however slight, can be given of Blake's symbolism here. It is exceedingly unlikely that anyone will possess a copy of the present reproductions of the Songs who has not made some acquaintance with the interpretation of the entire symbolic system prepared by the present writer in collaboration with Mr. Yeats, and printed in the first two volumes of the only complete edition of Blake's works,—that issued by the publisher of this facsimile. In those pages, the chapter on the Songs was very brief. Its substance will be found repeated here, with several additions. Like all the interpretation it was written then, and is re-written now, with some regret. No one willingly or cheerfully proposes to a reader and lover of Blake to turn away from the pleasure of the poetry and harass his mind by studying a prose explanation of the meaning. Yet such annoyance as is felt in the study of the vast net-work of myth and symbol to which every phrase is more or less related, turns to greater pleasure in the end. Presently the irritation of searching and comparing passes and is forgotten, while the effect remains. Then, instead of finding that the poetry of the poems has been frightened away by the symbolism, the reader perceives it to sing with a triple music; for now to the melody of the words and of the images is added a newer, sweeter, deeper cadence of magic potency.

Innocence and Experience are contrasted with one another because Blake's religious feelings forbade him to contrast Innocence and Guilt. To do so was to take up the method of Satan—the Accuser. There is no sin like the sin of accusation, because there is nothing so truly characteristic of the great Enemy. This, Blake firmly believed. In practice he was sometimes hurried into forgetting his creed. But in literature at least he attempted from the very first to remain faithful to it. Even apart from the idea of guilt, Experience—the knowledge of Good and Evil—is already so great a contrast to Innocence that Paradise cannot contain it.

In taking this title Blake gives the sign that his true career has begun. He is no longer, as in the Poetical Sketches, producing mere literature, however fresh, beautiful, and powerful. He is, from henceforward, not a poet among the poets—one singer more, where many were found before him. He begins to take his separate place as, above all things, the Teacher.

There is no necessary opposition between teaching and poetry as there is between innocence and experience. It happens, by evil fortune, that our Western teachers, even when they possess poetic power, lose it as a general rule when they begin to teach. The lesson enters, like Poverty at the door, and the poetry flies away like Love out of the window. But there is nothing of an abiding law, a fulfilment of the inherent nature of things, in this usual result of trying to convey doctrine with verse. It is a very strange and dreadful misfortune, and never loses its strangeness and repulsiveness, however often it may be repeated. It is also a puzzle that never ceases its bewilderment. Why should a man descend to prose the moment he begins to teach? There seems no reason for it. The natural expectation would be all the other way, did not common experience check our hopes while yet half formed. We should, if we had never read an improving verse, naturally expect a finer and more full-breathed melody from a singer who poured out his beloved and believed convictions on all great themes in the red-hot fury of proselytizing zeal.

Blake was never so full of poetry as when brimming over with doctrine. Should anyone be depressed by the faded and scentless rhymes of a teacher here, or a teacher there, until he is inclined to become himself the worst and most prosaic of all by giving forth as a critical law the absurd maxim that poetry should not teach, because teaching is unsuited to poetry—Blake is here to put him to shame and silence.

The very first lesson the Songs contain is in itself sufficient to account for their unfailing poetic spring, all doctrinal though they be. For it teaches the very method of the making of such song, and is, in fact, Blake's one great, if brief, Essay on Poetry. It tells us how the poet went piping *songs* down a valley. The pipe is of all instruments the early and elementary type of wordless music. But the poet already gave forth songs, while as yet he only used the pipe. The intention is the life in these things. He meant what he piped for songs, and they were songs. A child on a cloud understood him and even ordered a song to be piped on a definite subject—a song about a Lamb. Not until the poet had done this was he bid to drop his pipe and sing, and then to write the songs. Here, then, is the order of the generation of these poems. First, the intention, then the melody, then the words, and finally the recording pen. Do all poets with a purpose allow their songs to grow into existence through this healthful and natural order of change? Do they not habitually begin with the pen? The secret of the difference between Blake and so many others is not far to seek. But the process of making songs does not tell us all about them. We should know something of the ancestry of the convictions and emotions from which the very meaning has its birth. The reader takes the songs first, and if he enjoys them, may perhaps care to look for a meaning afterwards. But the poet began with the meaning, which first took the form of songs by love of the musical impulse, itself a part of the same mind,—an Eve of the otherwise childless Adam. In Blake's poetry the meaning is easy to find when once we know the man. He did not often write obscurely. Twenty-five years ago, Mr. Swinburne said in his really magnificent essay on Blake, which has every merit except interpretation, and will sometimes even partly unlock the magical secret which it praises so generously :—

"It is pleasant enough to commend and enjoy the palpable excellence of Blake's work; but another thing is simply and thoroughly requisite—to understand what the workman was after. First get well hold of the mystic and you will then at once get a better view of the painter and poet. And if through fear of tedium or offence a student refuses to be at such pains, he will find himself, while following Blake's trace as a poet and painter, brought up sharply within a very short tether."—P. 127.

Mr. Swinburne himself confesses that he was not sufficiently "at such pains" as he recommends. The same Essay says of this Mystic of whom we are "to get well hold":—

"The main part of him was, and is yet, simply inexplicable; much like some among his own designs, a maze of cloudy colour and perverse form, without a clue for the hand or a feature for the eye to lay hold of."—P. 4.

From the effort to comprehend him

"—— all mere human patience or comprehension recoils and reels back."

In the complete edition of the Works this "main part" has been relieved of its incomprehensibility once for all, and that most certainly by no greater or higher quality than "mere human patience." But it may not be quite waste of time now to sketch in a very few words an outline of Blake's view of what man truly is, that his conception of "the two contrary states of the human soul" may be indicated correctly, however broadly.

We are from eternity, Blake believed, real spirits—so independent of the sequence of Time and Space that the very word *from*, when used before *eternity*, is almost a mistake. We have in us a capacity of vitalizing a portion of ourselves, not used before birth, called the Body—actually a phase of mind fathered by Time and mothered by Space, solidified by the Five Senses. It is our danger as well as our delight. Through it our emotions take on an intensity needful for our eternal growth, while our minds are apt to succumb to the deceit of Reason (as we arrogantly call the mere "ratio of the Five Senses") until we "forget eternity." This narrow, bodily or restrictive portion of mind will die and be dissipated with our decomposition after death. It is not wanted in eternity. Here Blake spoke with the materialists who consider thought as a function of the brain. But an effect remains. There is a something in us, *not* our temporary reason or senses. The only part of us now belonging to it is the visionary power of the rare and clairvoyant Imagination. This takes food from the senses and the reason, but is deceived by neither. Though sensual joys and sensuous images and beliefs be "ruddy and sweet to eat," yet it knows that they are the "fruit of deceit"—as the song called the Human Abstract (No. 47) tells us. From the body springs egotism of all kinds, for this is born with the limited personality, and must die with it. Conscience, as a restrainer of this personality, and law and all that belongs to the Fall,—which was a fall from the eternal into the temporal state,—die with the phase of life with which they deal. But emotions, though also temporary, live, by means of their effect in producing sympathy, for sympathy is the apprenticeship through which we go before our pre-natal state regains its power of merging the One in the Everyone. Meantime we suffer, as well as enjoy. Our mortal part is framed in "cruelty," as well as in "deceit." The main business of life is to keep our minds open to imagination and brotherhood while going through the experience whose

2

danger is that it leads to materialistic reason and jealous individuality. To this end we should avoid the spirit that accuses more than we condemn the body that sins, and remember, even while we rebel against the darkness of nature, and its passions, that we could not endure all at once, without the shadow of that darkness—the terrific light which is to be given us eventually from the Fountain of Experience, though it be for a while disguised and seemingly withdrawn by the Fountain of Innocence.

Nowhere does Blake say all this at once, yet nowhere does he say anything else. He puts one side of the case and then another, as he allows voice after voice to sing separate songs, though he believed in the eventual merging which should make all voices and all men appear as one voice and one man. This one Man he calls Christ, for Christ when viewed as "The Door" is Imagination, while he is Emotion when viewed as "The Vine." Every mood and every truth within each of us is also a man, and when perverted from eternal purpose fights for its own little life and seeks to master its fellows and us, just as our selfishness would, if it could, teach us to master each other and God.

Many people have held views not unlike these. No other but Blake vivified the divided portions as a great myth, and lived for the uniting portion as a great purpose.

The Songs themselves may now be touched upon, each with but a word.

In the first we see the Shepherd. He is placed here as a type of the great emotional spirit watching over the little emotional morsels that are his flock. In him we may already see Tharmas—the Innocent Tharmas—for he also has two aspects, as a comparison of "Vala," Night IX., l. 384, &c., with "Milton," page 3, where he has become the "False Tongue," will show us. In the example of the Songs here copied, his blue coat indicates the region—(water)—to which he has mystic relations in the symbolic system. The "Lamb" preserves the same aspect and carries the image still further. With these the "Laughing Song," the "Cradle Song," the first "Holy Thursday," "Spring," the first "Nurse's Song" and "Infant's Joy" may be read. All refer to the flocks in their aspect of innocent happiness. Nothing is said about Tharmas by name. It is not certain that Blake himself knew, when he wrote the first portion of these Songs, what most of the names in his great myth would be. He never seems to have been proud of his own wonderful capacity of giving names to visionary forms. On the contrary, he seems to be surprised when one appears without telling its own name, as in the song "Infant Joy."

But even among the flocks there is not only infant joy, but infant sorrow ("Vala," Night IX., l. 549), which does not always understand itself. The "Little Boy Lost," and found, does not know that he is the "Little Black Boy," who is taught by his mother the meaning of mortal shadows. This teaching by the mother is a very rare incident in Blake's work. But the Innocent Mother, like all innocence, has her own wisdom. She is the contrary of Rahab, of whom so much is told in "Vala" and "Jerusalem." The picture has its counterpart in "America," page 14.

"Night" is the night of Nature, the period of our eternal lives when the lions of selfish passion have most power over the lambs of innocent passion, before the "new worlds" which these "mild spirits" shall inherit change the furious spirits from evil strength to strength without evil. The doctrine is the reverse of the preaching of asceticism or of Puritanism. The change in the "new worlds" does not merely regenerate the lion. It justifies him in having been first generated. Each "world" is a mood, one of those personal "states" into which the soul enters as it goes on its eternal voyage. In this poem, the sun descending in the West, and the golden tears of the re-born lion, are related to the mystic and mythic system of all the later books; as a comparison with "Vala," Night VI., l. 258, "Europe," pages 3 and 4, and other places will show. During this "night" when the lions and tigers "animal forms of wisdom" (" Vala," Night IX., 701, 830) "rush dreadful," Luvah in the myth assumes Urizen's world. The lion is afterwards called Rintrah, a portion of Urizen and of Luvah. The subject can only be traced when all the stories of the Zoas are considered. Then the harmony of these symbols with the expression "world" and other terms in the song will be seen in full symbolic value. The Zoas are explained, and their stories traced out and collected in the edition of the "Works" already referred to.

The "Divine Image" is a kind of sequel to the "Little Boy Found." When he was "lost" he merely pursued a vapour, which is shown in the picture as a vague little figure, just shapely enough to be seen as head-downwards,— an attitude afterwards explained in the Prophetic Books, and expressive of the state of man when following reason only. It is, however, a light of a kind, though not of the sufficient kind. God, though pictured here as the Angel of Pity, appears only "like his father," to the little boy,—who becomes "found" in the act of perceiving the Divine Image. The last lines of the "Auguries of Innocence" (see Works,—Vol. III., p. 79) partly explain this from the visionary point of view.

> " We are led to believe a lie
> When we see *with* not *through* the eye,
> Which was born in a night, to perish in a night
> When the soul slept in beams of light.
> God appears and God is light
> To those poor souls who dwell in night,
> But doth a human form display
> To those who dwell in realms of day."

In the last line of the first Holy Thursday, "Pity" is seen as "an angel,"—

2 *

a portion of God, in separated form. Even in the "Dream" the glowworm is human. It is represented in the margin as a watchman with lantern and staff. Of human insects we hear also in "Vala," Night IX., lines 738, &c., in "Milton," p. 24, &c. "Man looks out in tree, and herb, and fish, and beast," as we are told in "Vala," Night VIII., 1. 553, &c., for these contain the "scattered" portions of his immortal body. They are all, in fact, Little Boys Lost in their way.

"On Another's Sorrow," goes on with "Night." Humanity, or God, who "suffers with those that suffer" (Jerusalem, p. 25, l. 7), here "sits beside" them, as he does in the forms of Angels, in "Night." This is placed among the Songs of Innocence to make evident the doctrine that sorrow is not necessarily a punishment inflicted. It is an initiation, among other things. In our modern Protestant Christianity, Judgment plays so large a part that we sometimes look on the idea that all suffering must necessarily be punitive as though this were an essential part of a belief in Divine Justice. The Catholic Church still reminds us that there is another view of pain. She holds up the image of the Virgin Mary with seven swords in her breast, while preaching the doctrine that her wounds were no punishment for her own short-comings, for she was born free, even of the taint of "original sin," while they were still less a vicarious sacrifice;—that of her Son being complete in itself.

Blake has the clearest view of the purpose of sorrow. In "Jerusalem," p. 38, fallen man (fallen into the deceived state of unimaginative and selfish convictions) is followed by the Divine Saviour who :—

"Display'd the Eternal Vision, the Divine Similitude
In loves and tears of brothers, sisters, sons, fathers, and friends,
Which if Man ceases to behold he ceases to exist."

In passing now to the Songs of Experience we enter altogether a new region. It is understood now that we are in the state when the soul has "lapsed" in the evening dew. Five years have passed since the Songs of Innocence were written, perhaps even more, for the date, 1789, on their title-page represents the year when the plates were engraved, not necessarily that of the composition of the poems. The Songs of Experience bear date 1794. They may have been written from time to time during the whole of this period. These five years saw an important ripening of Blake's mind. It is the habit of those whose acquaintance with his works is but slight to speak as though the "Songs of Innocence and Experience" were a single set of poems, belonging to the early, or as they fancy, the sane period of Blake's life, while the "Prophetic Books" and all the symbolic writings are to be classed as mere ravings, the result of a falling away of a once bright and promising intellect. But the year 1789 is not only the date of the Songs of Innocence, but also of the Book of Thel, though a broken letter has caused the date to seem to be 1780 in the facsimile given in the "Works,"—while 1790 saw the "Marriage of Heaven and Hell" engraved. "Tiriel" is supposed by some critics to be as early, or earlier, though its date has not been fixed. The "Vision of the Daughters of Albion," with its motto "The eye sees more than the heart knows," was printed in 1793; so was "America," and "Europe." The "Gates of Paradise" belong to the same year. The "Ghost of Abel" claims, in a footnote of Blake's own, that the "original stereotype" belonged to 1780,—though this is difficult to believe;—here also the last figure should perhaps be 9.

It is not surprising that the Songs of Experience begin with a very different note from that of the Songs of Innocence. Even if we suppose that when he wrote the former, Blake was only partly conscious of the full scope of his visionary poetic message, there can be no doubt that it had been in great measure revealed to him before he collected the second portion of what is too often looked on as one work.

The voice of the Ancient Bard, who speaks through Blake, calls on Earth to "return." The meaning is that she should re-enter the state of innocence by the door of forgiveness.

> "Mutual forgiveness of each vice,
> Such are the gates of Paradise."

As he says in the poem of the Gates. Every word is symbolic in these first Songs of Experience. The evening dew is the pity that joins what wrath separates, the ancient Word walks in the evening,—the moment when the soul falls into the Night of Nature, and calls on her to seek the inspired life by casting off the worship of law. It bids her cease to know good and evil,— to disgorge from the spirit's choked throat the deadly apple that stops the pure breath of eternity. The starry floor—thought, and the watery shore,—emotion are given to the lapsed soul. But she believes that she is given to them, and so ceases to be able to control the axis of the mind,—the starry pole,—and renew the light of inspiration, fallen into the darkness of reason.

Earth demands to be relieved from the restrictions of the body that oblige her spirit to know of love through the flesh—an evil as great as though the ploughman were compelled to plough in darkness and the seedsman sow by night. This restriction is the "cruel" work of that "selfish Father of men," who is no other than Satan, Prince of this world—often worshipped as God—so the Prophetic Books remind us. Meanwhile, one evil breeds another. Dark flesh breeds dark law, and the chain of jealousy, called morality, even freezes around the bones in whose cage we must needs learn what of love we may.

Naturally, there are two sorts of love in us, as there are two selves. The clod and the pebble, soft dark earth and hard dark earth, tell each other of the two loves in the next poem. Even children are made prisoners to cold charity, as our infant emotions are to the chill restraints that hardly allow them food. A spiritual Holy Thursday utters this terrible complaint and reproach. Those who would break through the bondage are lost. A little girl—a soft, feminine emotion—goes wandering among the wild-beast passions. But they are good to her, for she is no accuser of sin. Yet her parents mourn and seek her, believing that evil will come to her. Yet when they go where she is (when do parents in real life make this journey?) they also find that what was called evil and destruction is neither the one nor the other. But when once they have allowed sympathy to take them to the desert, there must be no return if they are to live fearless, while the wolves and lions howl and growl. The lion, it will be noted, is here distinctly said to be himself a " vision."

Then follow songs in the voice, not of the clod, but of the pebble. Mere selfishness is unmasked in the suffering inflicted on the Chimney Sweeper. The Nurse, moved by envy, not by care for their good, seeks to put a stop to the playing of children, and the worm of jealousy destroys the crimson joy of the Sick Rose.

As a relief comes the little song of the Fly. Symbolism goes to sleep. A plain suggestion as to what life and death are takes its place. But if

> " The want
> Of thought is death,"

then, in a certain sense, we are always in that state, for none think with perfect vividness. But Blake, for once, does not limit the application of his question. Yet if we wish to know what else was in his mind as he wrote this we must read again the lines

> " Art not thou
> A man like me ? "

along with the passages already referred to about the human form, even of insects, and this from " Milton," p. 18, l. 27 :—

> " Seest thou the little winged fly smaller than a grain of sand ?
> It has a heart like thee, a brain open to heaven and hell,
> Withinside wondrous and expansive. Its gates are not closed.
> I hope thine are not. Hence it clothes itself in rich array."

In " the Angel," the story of youth arming itself with modesty and hiding from its own spirit the delight of its own heart, until the helplessness of old age makes all arming and hiding unneeded, requires no explanation. The question at the beginning remains. What can it mean? Why does the body thus cheat the spirit—why does the body make us believe that it exists at all, imposing its "little curtain of flesh" upon the bed of our soul's desire? It is the question that in the last lines of the book of Thel resounds from emotion's grave and drives it in terror from earth.

The Tiger brings out a belief of Blake's that the direct acts of creation were not all performed by one personal God in His own and undivided character, but were given out in commission to minor portions of Himself, each a god in its way. Of these, some were contraries of others in character. Of course, the Tiger is a mood. He is one of those "Tigers of wrath" who are "wiser than the horses of discretion," as we are told in the "Marriage of Heaven and Hell." He is said to roam, not in the night of the forest, it will be noted, but in the forests of the night, in the doubts and difficulties and melancholy of mortal existence.

The third verse is difficult to explain as it stands. Perhaps Blake thought it would do, as possibly meaning

> "And what shoulder and what art
> Could twist the sinews of thy heart,
> And when thy heart began to beat,
> What dread hand and what dread feet (could twist them ?)."

But in his original manuscript the poem ran thus—

> "What dread hand and what dread feet
> Could fetch it from the furnace deep,
> And in thy horrid ribs dare steep,
> In the well of sanguine woe?"

The stanza was never completed, and the three lines omitted when the song was engraved, without any alteration of that which preceded. Blake seems to have been groping uncertainly after his final form of expression. All the various readings will be found in the "Works," Vol. III., pp. 91 and 92.

In the "Pretty Rose Tree," jealousy shows us the meaning of the "Worm" in the Sick Rose. The Sunflower repeats the craving of youth and sighs for its satisfaction in eternity where the sun, the traveller of time, ends his journey.

The Lily claims that the most perfect love shall be considered to share, as of right, one symbol with the most perfect purity. (Is not this, considered merely as four lines of verse, the most beautiful quatrain in the English language?)

In the Garden of Love, the Natural Man is heard protesting against the moral claims that asceticism has imposed on the world through religion.

In the "Little Vagabond" Blake preaches again the total repudiation of all accusation of sin, of all punishment, and of all restriction. That this doctrine is contained in Christianity, along with its balancing contrary, the love of God and one's neighbour, is, of course, no new contention, but Blake's care was to show how dogmatic morality in religion actually tends, not to righteousness, but rather to more rebellion. This rebellion, he believed, would lead ultimately to the love of God and neighbour, while the dogma and moral law led to neither the one nor the other. Therefore he would make a clean sweep, not only of all law, but even of all disapprobation. In "Jerusalem," p. 3, he says :—

> "Therefore I print, nor vain my types shall be,
> Heaven, Earth, and Hell henceforth shall live in harmony."

In "London" the failure of restrictive law to give any energy to the real life or love of the soul is indignantly declared.

The "Human Abstract" is a lyrical epitome of many pages in the prophetic Books. The story and meaning of the person called "Urizen" in the myth is here to be found foreshadowed, but without the name. The "Book of Urizen" has the same date as the Songs of Experience.

Infant Sorrow is the companion to Infant Joy and repeats the story of the "Human Abstract" in its infantile form. This is the Natural Man, the mortal. His personality is purely selfish,—a fiend. His visible body, the cloud, hides it. His father, type of law and repression, is himself the maturity of mundane reason. His mother is the maturity of instinct, less cruel his soul, save deceitfully, as helping to solidify his body. These three persons, all of them living at one time in each of us, are continually recurring in Blake's myth. They are developed at length in the story of Los, Enitharmon, and Orc.

In the "Poison Tree" Blake gives one of his few sarcastic poems. There is little symbolism here. The Tree is the inevitable "Mystery" in one of its aspects. The parable repeats the doctrine that all suppression of impulse or truth is evil. It develops the saying from the "Marriage of Heaven and Hell," that "the voice of honest indignation is the voice of God," by showing, in contrast, the silence of dishonest submissiveness growing into the vindictive secrecy of Satan. It was probably based on an incident, the theft of some design of Blake's by a brother artist.

"A little boy lost" tells of an honest love destroyed by the pride and arrogance of the being to whom it was offered. It is a variation of the parable of Lear and Cordelia. "So young, my Lord, and true." Symbolically it shows old Reason jealously binding young Imagination.

"A little girl lost" is also an honest young love destroyed, but this time the destroyer is not consciously cruel and suffers also, for the "girl" is a fleshly instinctive emotion of his own, at variance with the white self-submissive hair of virtue, strong for the easy task of disapproval, but weak for the harder effort of sympathy and forgiveness.

"To Tirzah" condenses a whole volume of mysticism. It accepts mortality for the five senses and is glad of it, since they are the source both of error and pain. It gives the mystic view of the Redemption, and asserts the immortality of Imagination,—or Jesus. Every word here is in the language of the "Prophetic Books," and a full account of these few stanzas would include almost a complete analysis of their symbolic system.

"The Schoolboy" usually included by Blake among the Songs of Innocence, comes in odd contrast from its simplicity. It is mere literature, without symbolism,—a picturesque plea for freedom and nothing else. The horn heard on a summer's morn, and attributed to a distant huntsman, was probably a harvest horn such as is still used in the Thames valley to call labourers to the field in the early morning. It is not unlikely that Blake during one of his early country walks heard the horn and not knowing that the hunting season was over, nor seeing where the sound came from, mistakenly assumed that the note proved the existence of the distant hunt-man.

In the end Blake utters his favourite claim for poetic inspiration as being a better and truer guide for life than argument and troublesome searchings into natural fact. In his essay on Chaucer's Canterbury Pilgrims, printed in the Descriptive Catalogue, he describes how, in his own picture, he represents Chaucer riding beside the Clerk of Oxenford "as if the youthful clerk had put himself under the tuition of the mature poet," and adds, "Let the Philosopher always be the servant and scholar of inspiration and all will be happy."

THE ILLUSTRATIONS.

It is not surprising that the different examples of the Songs differ from one another in the colouring of the pictures and of the entire pages of text. During the long space of time between 1789 and 1827, whenever he was in want of money and no employment of engraving or designing presented itself, Blake would tint and sell a volume of the Songs. The earlier in date the slighter, and sometimes the cruder were the tints. There are some exceptions to this, a few early examples being of most delicate beauty. At first the outlines and text were printed in a very dark grey colour, almost black. Then red ink was adopted.

Blake never intended the rough outlines which he prepared as anything but guides to his own hand in colouring the plates. He did not invariably follow them even as guides, but would vary the size of the plate at the edges and alter the less important details to please his own mood. In the great majority of these plates the facsimile here given is from the actual outline as used by Blake. He drew in stopping-out varnish on plain copper or zinc,

3

and then dissolved away with acid all the rest of the surface, so that the outlines stood up, and could be printed from like types. Those pages where a little shading of a mossy kind is to be seen are photographed from copies already coloured by Blake, and the result printed in monochrome. In these cases no uncoloured original was accessible for re-production. The shading is due to the fact that a little of the colour-effect always united itself to the outline.

A complete facsimile, hand-coloured, has been issued. The outlines being the same as those here printed. A very limited number have been executed.

The symbolism of the illustrations is not very marked in most places. The flames on the title-page are obviously the clothing of

"—— burning fires
And unsatisfied desires."

The trees always refer to "Mystery," as that on page 3 with a serpent wound round it, hardly distinguishable from the bark, indicates. The figures on page 4 are so slight as to be almost incomprehensible; they seem to represent, if one reads them from top to bottom of the page, first on the left and then on the right :—

1. An old person teaching a child.
2. A nude girl leaping from a tree. (? Spring.)
3 and 4. Robed figures turning the leaves of very large books or rolls.
5. The lark mounting. (A subject symbolically used in the book called " Milton.")
6. A robed figure reading.
7. A woman sowing corn in a field, or feeding flying birds.
8. A shepherdess sitting holding a crook up in the right hand.

The appropriateness is clear enough, though they can hardly be said to illustrate the particular poem in every case.

The grapes on pages 6 and 7 are clearly symbolic and refer to the "vegetative happy" state of youth.

No. 9 shows the serpent round the tree again, as on the title-page. In the contrasted picture in "America" the serpent comes from the woman herself, as in the biblical figure in Revelations. No. 10 shows a scene representing youth taught beneath a tree, but here the serpent is changed into a lily, and grows upright from the root. In No. 11, the Blossoms, Sparrows and Robins *all* have human form, and their emotional meaning is as clear as that of the flame-like tree where they cluster. In 12, the subject is clear enough, and in 13, though the little boy lost is so like a little girl. In 14, the angel who leads him is more female than male. The figure, as already suggested, is probably the Angel of God's Pity, and the spiritual likeness of that mood of the boy's father only. In the facsimile of this plate the boy's face was hardly possible to imitate, being a failure in the original,—a few ugly dots placed, perhaps on a dark day, in an almost shapeless round mass.

In No. 15, the illustration hints that children are to be understood symbolically rather than realistically as the audience chosen for the Songs, for here are full-grown youths and maidens made childlike for once through the innocence of laughter, actually carousing in an arbour. A few years later Blake published his "Gates of Paradise," which Gilchrist says is inscribed in some copies as "For the Sexes," and in others "For Children."

The "Cradle Song" has no symbolism in its illustration, but in the "Divine Image" a scroll of flame, partly green, again compares vegetation with consuming fire, and at its roots the creation of Eve is indicated. The creator at the same moment lifts the newly wakened Adam by the hand towards the light. Above are seen figures in adoration, intended to be modern, for the light still shines. Other figures, seemingly angelic, encourage them.

The charity children in page 19 offer no enigma. "Night," on page 20, has a crouching form very roughly sketched at the foot of the tree to the right. It seems to be a lion with a human head,—a childish head,—but it is too small and slight to be anything but a subject for conjecture. The facsimile repeats the puzzle of the original accurately. On page 21, two figures see three in a group. All are holy. The subject is the advance from the dual state to the triad,—afterwards developed in the Prophetic Books.

"Spring" and the "Nurse's Song" may be passed, but the red lily on page 25 is evidently intended symbolically, for the "Infant Joy" is not placed in a flower of this colour at random. In the "Sick Rose" the words

> "—— thy bed
> Of crimson joy,"

leave no doubt of the symbol. The Dream has been referred to above with its human glowworm. Page 28 shows the group of page 2 with curious differences. The pipe has gone. The green robe of the shepherd is purple, and the child in the cloud has grown wings, and sits on his head. These should be the changes in the symbol when innocence is enriched by laughter, love, and song.

The Songs of Experience begin with a picture which reminds us that experience is death. The Introduction on page 30 in its nude woman on a cloud, shows the "Watery Shore" in human symbol. It is a different figure, but is, in its way, an aspect of Tharmas—the beginning of Innocence and of Experience. But there is no space here for the story of Tharmas, the third Zoa.

The serpent at the foot of Earth's Answer is almost an additional sentence to the song, so clearly does it show the source of all bondage. In the "Clod and the Pebble," the symbolic sheep and cattle that tread the clod are easy to understand. The frogs, worm, and duck drawn below, are elementary inhabitants of the watery world.

The "Infant Joys" who suffer in the pictures to the second Holy Thursday are shown as sad, but not attenuated children. They are not skeletons. They bear no visible imprint of hunger. Their cravings are emotional and spiritual.

The little girl lost is herself a desire in the bosom of a grown up maiden, who, in the picture, stands in a robe of "crimson joy," embracing her lover in sad slate colour, the two surrounded by a purple cloud, a portion of midnight, through which she points to the light. In the second picture she is alone, lying in despair under the trees, dressed in grey. Not a trace of direct connection with the story can be found, the object of the pictures being to explain the vision of the poem rather than to embody the description in the verse. This is done in the last design to "A Little Girl Found," where innocence and passion are seen in happy companionship, evidently in the "new worlds" of the Song called "Night." The rough sketch, apparently from life, of the Chimney Sweep in a snow-storm, is valuable as showing how free Blake felt in putting down whatever made an impression on him, without asking himself for one moment whether the result would look decorative or poetic. The illustration to the second Nurse's Song shows a pretty girl in red—evidently the Nurse herself, in the lost "days of her youth"—stopping to admire the head of a romantic boy in green, who strikes an attitude and waits for her to go on combing his hair.

In great contrast, the next picture, showing the soul of the sick rose taking flight as the worm crawls in, is so simple a symbol that explanation is silent before it, because it is so easy to explain. But the picture to the Fly renews interpretative difficulty. What have the nurse, the little boy, and the girl with the battledore and shuttlecock to do with the poem? These children are "happy flies." The Angel and the Maiden Queen bring us back to the region of the obvious again, as does the absurd tiger who spoils the page of a fine poem. The Pretty Rose Tree shows the red girl and the slate-coloured lover of a former picture, and suggests their meaning.

In the next, the monk and two children by an open grave are an addition to the poem, not only an illustration. They show the "happy flies" unnecessarily saddened when caught in the "net of religion."

The "Little Vagabond" with its audaciously prosaic and bewilderingly blunt language, is cruelly placed below the finest of all the designs, representing the great reconciliation, that of God and Adam, in whose bosom is the "Devil" to whom the poem wishes "drink and apparel." They kneel to each other, one in contrition, the Other in pity.

"London" shows London personated as an old man "blind and age-bent, begging through the streets of Babylon, led by a child." Instinct or innocence guiding worn-out reason through the mazes of morality, one of Blake's favourite subjects. The drawing is repeated in "Jerusalem," p. 84.

Urizen in his net,—reason caught by religion,—is shown in the next design. This net means restrictive, not inspired religion, as we read in the story of Urizen in the prophetic books,—a view showing more originality and genius in its day, a hundred years ago, than we can, without effort, realize now. The picture to "Infant Sorrow" shows a child apparently reaching out towards a dream that eludes its grasp while a kind mother offers it unwelcome affection in place of golden imaginings. This again is a continuation and not only an illustration of the poem.

The corpse under the poison tree illustrates the next verses exactly, but leaves all that is obscure in them just where it was. The same may be said of the picture to "A Little Boy Lost."

The poem "To Tirzah" ends with a design that continues it—two females helplessly supporting a dying man. They are in red and grey, and show the temporary emotions, sad and glad, that are now of no avail. God the father brings him the waters of life. That there might be no error as to the effect the draught will produce, Blake has printed on his garments the warning of St. Paul against all misconception about the resurrection:—"It is raised a spiritual body." After the little sketch of schoolboys playing at marbles that follows, comes the figure of the Bard, like that of the Father, and like the "father" mentioned in the Song of Innocence, "The Little Boy Lost," in white. This is the image of the "Ancient Word." It is not impossible that both these poems —"The Schoolboy" and "The Voice of the Ancient Bard"—appear here by accident or oversight, they are included among the "Songs of Innocence" in some earlier other examples. Blake frequently altered the order of his pages, and it is not always easy to be sure of his reasons for doing so.

SONGS
of
INNOCENCE
and Of
EXPERIENCE

Shewing the Two Contrary States
of the Human Soul

SONGS
of
Innocence

1789

The Author & Printer W Blake.

Introduction

Piping down the valleys wild
Piping songs of pleasant glee
On a cloud I saw a child.
And he laughing said to me

Pipe a song about a Lamb
So I piped with merry chear,
Piper pipe that song again
So I piped he wept to hear.

Drop thy pipe thy happy pipe
Sing thy songs of happy chear
So I sung the same again
While he wept with joy to hear

Piper sit thee down and write
In a book that all may read
So he vanishd from my sight
And I pluckd a hollow reed

And I made a rural pen,
And I staind the water clear,
And I wrote my happy songs,
Every child may joy to hear.

The Shepherd.

How sweet is the Shepherds sweet lot!
From the morn to the evening he strays.
He shall follow his sheep all the day
And his tongue shall be filled with praise.

For he hears the lambs innocent call.
And he hears the ewes tender reply.
He is watchful while they are in peace,
For they know when their Shepherd is nigh.

6

The Ecchoing Green

The Sun does arise,
And make happy the skies;
The merry bells ring
To welcome the Spring;
The sky-lark and thrush,
The birds of the bush,
Sing louder around,
To the bells chearful sound,
While our sports shall be seen
On the Ecchoing Green.

Old John with white hair
Does laugh away care,
Sitting under the oak,
Among the old folk,

They

They laugh at our play,
And soon they all say,
Such such were the joys
When we all girls & boys
In our youth we were seen
On the Echoing Green.

Till the little ones weary
No more can be merry
The sun does descend,
And our sports have an end.
Round the laps of their mothers
Many sisters and brothers,
Like birds in their nest
Are ready for rest,
And sport no more seen
On the darkening green.

8

The Lamb

Little Lamb who made thee
Dost thou know who made thee
Gave thee life & bid thee feed.
By the stream & o'er the mead;
Gave thee clothing of delight,
Softest clothing wooly bright;
Gave thee such a tender voice,
Making all the vales rejoice:
Little Lamb who made thee
Dost thou know who made thee

Little Lamb I'll tell thee,
Little Lamb I'll tell thee;
He is called by thy name,
For he calls himself a Lamb:
He is meek & he is mild,
He became a little child:
I a child & thou a lamb,
We are called by his name.
Little Lamb God bless thee,
Little Lamb God bless thee.

9

The Little Black Boy

My mother bore me in the southern wild,
And I am black, but O! my soul is white
White as an angel is the English child:
But I am black as if bereav'd of light.

My mother taught me underneath a tree
And sitting down before the heat of day.
She took me on her lap and kissed me,
And pointing to the east began to say.

Look on the rising sun: there God does live
And gives his light and gives his heat away.
And flowers and trees and beasts and men recieve
Comfort in morning joy in the noon day.

And we are put on earth a little space,
That we may learn to bear the beams of love.
And these black bodies and this sun-burnt face
Is but a cloud and like a shady grove.

For

10

For when our souls have learn'd the heat to bear
The cloud will vanish we shall hear his voice
Saying: come out from the grove my love & care
And round my golden tent like lambs rejoice.

Thus did my mother say and kissed me,
And thus I say to little English boy.
When I from black and he from white cloud free,
And round the tent of God like lambs we joy:

Ill shade him from the heat till he can bear,
To lean in joy upon our fathers knee
And then Ill stand and stroke his silver hair
And be like him and he will then love me

The Blossom.

Merry Merry Sparrow
Under leaves so green
A happy Blossom
Sees you swift as arrow
Seek your cradle narrow
Near my Bosom.

Pretty Pretty Robin
Under leaves so green
A happy Blossom
Hears you sobbing sobbing
Pretty Pretty Robin
Near my Bosom

12

The Chimney Sweeper

When my mother died I was very young,
And my father sold me while yet my tongue,
Could scarcely cry weep weep weep weep.
So your chimneys I sweep & in soot I sleep.

Theres little Tom Dacre who cried when his head
That curld like a lambs back, was shavd, so I said
Hush Tom never mind it for when your heads bare.
You know that the soot cannot spoil your white hair.

And so he was quiet, & that very night,
As Tom was a sleeping he had such a sight,
That thousands of sweepers Dick, Joe, Ned & Jack
Were all of them lock'd up in coffins of black,

And by came an Angel who had a bright key
And he opend the coffins & set them all free.
Then down a green plain leaping laughing they run
And wash in a river and shine in the Sun.

Then naked & white, all their bags left behind
They rise upon clouds, and sport in the wind.
And the Angel told Tom if he'd be a good boy.
He'd have God for his father & never want joy.

And so Tom awoke and we rose in the dark
And got with our bags & our brushes to work.
Tho the morning was cold, Tom was happy & warm,
So if all do their duty, they need not fear harm.

The Little Boy lost

Father, father where are you going
O do not walk so fast.
Speak father, speak to your little boy
Or else I shall be lost,

The night was dark no father was there
The child was wet with dew.
The mire was deep, & the child did weep
And away the vapour flew.

The Little Boy found

The little boy lost in the lonely fen,
Led by the wandring light,
Began to cry but God ever nigh,
Appeard like his father in white.

He kissed the child & by the hand led
And to his mother brought,
Who in sorrow pale. thro' the lonely dale
Her little boy weeping sought.

Laughing Song.

When the green woods laugh with the voice of joy
And the dimpling stream runs laughing by,
When the air does laugh with our merry wit,
And the green hill laughs with the noise of it.

When the meadows laugh with lively green,
And the grasshopper laughs in the merry scene,
When Mary and Susan and Emily.
With their sweet round mouths sing Ha, Ha, He.

When the painted birds laugh in the shade
Where our table with cherries and nuts is spread
Come live & be merry and join with me,
To sing the sweet chorus of Ha Ha, He.

16

A CRADLE SONG

Sweet dreams form a shade
O'er my lovely infants head:
Sweet reams of pleasant streams,
By happy silent moony beams

Sweet sleep with soft down.
Weave thy brows an infant crown.
Sweet sleep Angel mild,
Hover o'er my happy child.

Sweet smiles in the night.
Hover over my delight.
Sweet smiles Mothers smiles
All the livelong night beguiles.

Sweet moans, dovelike sighs,
Chase not slumber from thy eyes.
Sweet moans, sweeter smiles,
All the dovelike moans beguiles.

Sleep sleep happy child.
All creation slept and smil'd.
Sleep sleep, happy sleep.
While o'er thee thy mother weep

Sweet babe in thy face.
Holy image I can trace.
Sweet babe once like thee.
Thy maker lay and wept for me

Wept!

Wept for me for thee for all.
When he was an infant small.
Thou his image ever see
Heavenly face that smiles on thee

Smiles on thee on me on all
Who became an infant small
Infant smiles are his own smiles
Heaven & earth to peace beguiles

The Divine Image

To Mercy Pity Peace and Love
All pray in their distress:
And to these virtues of delight
Return their thankfulness.

For Mercy Pity Peace and Love,
Is God our father dear:
And Mercy Pity Peace and Love,
Is Man his child and care.

For Mercy has a human heart
Pity, a human face:
And Love, the human form divine,
And Peace, the human dress.

Then every man of every clime,
That prays in his distress,
Prays to the human form divine
Love Mercy Pity Peace.

And all must love the human form,
In heathen, turk or jew.
Where Mercy, Love & Pity dwell,
There God is dwelling too.

19

HOLY THURSDAY

'Twas on a Holy Thursday their innocent faces clean,
The children walking two & two in red & blue & green
Grey headed beadles walkd before with wands as white as snow
Till into the high dome of Pauls they like Thames waters flow

O what a multitude they seemd these flowers of London town
Seated in companies they sit with radiance all their own
The hum of multitudes was there but multitudes of lambs
Thousands of little boys & girls raising their innocent hands

Now like a mighty wind they raise to heaven the voice of song
Or like harmonious thunderings the seats of heaven among
Beneath them sit the aged men wise guardians of the poor,
Then cherish pity, lest you drive an angel from your door.

20

Night

The sun descending in the west.
The evening star does shine.
The birds are silent in their nest,
And I must seek for mine.
The moon like a flower,
In heavens high bower;
With silent delight,
Sits and smiles on the night.

Farewell green fields and happy groves,
Where flocks have took delight.
Where lambs have nibbled, silent moves
The feet of angels bright:
Unseen they pour blessing,
And joy without ceasing,
On each bud and blossom,
And each sleeping bosom.

They look in every thoughtless nest.
Where birds are coverd warm;
They visit caves of every beast,
To keep them all from harm:
If they see any weeping,
That should have been sleeping
They pour sleep on their head
And sit down by their bed.

21

When wolves and tygers howl for prey
They pitying stand and weep;
Seeking to drive their thirst away,
And keep them from the sheep.
But if they rush dreadful,
The angels most heedful,
Recieve each mild spirit,
New worlds to inherit.

And there the lions ruddy eyes,
Shall flow with tears of gold:
And pitying the tender cries,
And walking round the fold:
Saying, wrath by his meekness
And by his health. sickness
Is driven away.
From our immortal day.

And now beside thee bleating lamb,
I can lie down and sleep;
Or think on him who bore thy name,
Grace after thee and weep.
For wash'd in lifes river,
My bright mane for ever,
Shall shine like the gold,
As I guard o'er the fold.

Spring

Sound the Flute!
Now its mute
Birds delight
Day and Night.
Nightingale
In the dale
Lark in Sky
Merrily
Merrily Merrily to welcome in the Year

Little Boy
Full of joy .

Little

Little Girl
Sweet and small.
Cock does crow
So do you
Merry voice
Infant noise
Merrily. Merrily to welcome in the Year

Little Lamb
Here I am.
Come and lick
My white neck.
Let me pull
Your soft Wool.
Let me kiss
Your soft face.
Merrily Merrily we welcome in the Year

Nurses Song

When the voices of children are heard on the green
And laughing is heard on the hill
My heart is at rest within my breast
And every thing else is still

Then come home my children the sun is gone down
And the dews of night arise
Come come leave off play, and let us away
Till the morning appears in the skies

No no let us play, for it is yet day
And we cannot go to sleep
Besides in the sky, the little birds fly
And the hills are all coverd with sheep

Well well go & play till the light fades away
And then go home to bed
The little ones leaped & shouted & laugh'd
And all the hills ecchoëd

Infant Joy

I have no name
I am but two days old —
What shall I call thee?
I happy am
Joy is my name, —
Sweet joy befall thee!

Pretty joy!
Sweet joy but two days old,
Sweet joy I call thee:
Thou dost smile.
I sing the while
Sweet joy befall thee.

A Dream

Once a dream did weave a shade.
O'er my Angel-guarded bed.
That an Emmet lost its way
Where on grafs methought I lay.

Troubled wilderd and folorn
Dark benighted travel-worn.
Over many a tangled spray.
All heart-broke I heard her say.

O my children! do they cry.
Do they hear their father sigh.
Now they look abroad to see.
Now return and weep for me.

Pitying I dropd a tear:
But I saw a glow-worm near:
Who replied. What wailing wight
Calls the watchman of the night.

I am set to light the ground,
While the beetle goes his round:
Follow now the beetles hum,
Little wanderer hie thee home.

27

On Anothers Sorrow

Can I see anothers woe.
And not be in sorrow too
Can I see anothers grief.
And not seek for kind relief.

Can I see a falling tear
And not feel my sorrows share.
Can a father see his child.
Weep, nor be with sorrow filld.

Can a mother sit and hear.
An infant groan an infant fear—
No no never can it be.
Never never can it be.

And can he who smiles on all
Hear the wren with sorrows small.
Hear the small birds grief & care
Hear the woes that infants bear—

And not sit beside the nest
Pouring pity in their breast
And not sit the cradle near
Weeping tear on infants tear.

And not sit both night & day.
Wiping all our tears away.
O! no never can it be.
Never never can it be.

He doth give his joy to all.
He becomes an infant small.
He becomes a man of woe
He doth feel the sorrow too.

Think not, thou canst sigh a sigh
And thy maker is not by
Think not, thou canst weep a tear.
And thy maker is not near.

O! he gives to us his joy
That our grief he may destroy
Till our grief is fled & gone
He doth sit by us and moan

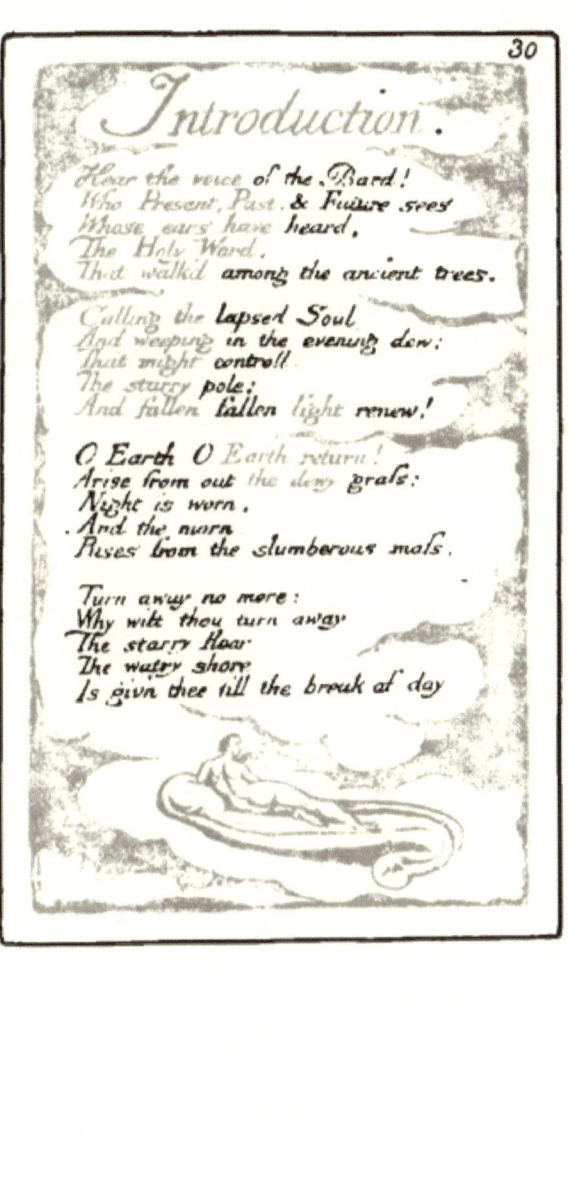

30

Introduction.

Hear the voice of the Bard!
Who Present, Past, & Future sees
Whose ears have heard,
The Holy Word,
That walk'd among the ancient trees.

Calling the lapsed Soul
And weeping in the evening dew:
That might controll
The starry pole;
And fallen fallen light renew!

O Earth O Earth return!
Arise from out the dewy grass;
Night is worn,
And the morn
Rises from the slumberous mass.

Turn away no more:
Why wilt thou turn away
The starry floor
The watry shore
Is given thee till the break of day

31

EARTH'S Answer.

Earth rais'd up her head.
From the darkness dread & drear.
Her light fled.
Stony dread!
And her locks cover'd with grey despair.

Prison'd on watry shore
Starry Jealousy does keep my den
Cold and hoar
Weeping o'er
I hear the father of the ancient men

Selfish father of man
Cruel jealous selfish fear
Can delight
Chain'd in night
The virgins of youth and morning bear.

Does spring hide its joy
When buds and blossoms grow?
Does the sower?
Sow by night?
Or the plowman in darkness plow?

Break this heavy chain
That does freeze my bones around
Selfish! vain!
Eternal bane!
That free Love with bondage bound.

32

The CLOD & the PEBBLE

Love seeketh not Itself to please,
Nor for itself hath any care;
But for another gives its ease,
And builds a Heaven in Hells despair.

So sung a little Clod of Clay,
Trodden with the cattles feet:
But a Pebble of the brook,
Warbled out these metres meet.

Love seeketh only Self to please,
To bind another to Its delight:
Joys in anothers loss of ease,
And builds a Hell in Heavens despite.

33

HOLY THURSDAY

Is this a holy thing to see,
In a rich and fruitful land,
Babes reduced to misery,
Fed with cold and usurous hand?

Is that trembling cry a song?
Can it be a song of joy?
And so many children poor?
It is a land of poverty!

And their sun does never shine,
And their fields are bleak & bare,
And their ways are fill'd with thorns,
It is eternal winter there.

For where-e'er the sun does shine,
And where-e'er the rain does fall:
Babe can never hunger there,
Nor poverty the mind appall.

The Little Girl Lost

In futurity
I prophetic see,
That the earth from sleep,
(Grave the sentence deep)

Shall arise and seek
For her maker meek:
And the desart wild
Become a garden mild.

In the southern clime,
Where the summers prime,
Never fades away;
Lovely Lyca lay.

Seven summers old
Lovely Lyca told,
She had wanderd long,
Hearing wild birds song.

Sweet sleep come to me
Underneath this tree;
Do father, mother weep.
Where can Lyca sleep.

Lost in desart wild
Is your little child
How can Lyca sleep,
If her mother weep.

If her heart does ake,
Then let Lyca wake;
If my mother sleep,
Lyca shall not weep,

Frowning frowning night,
O'er this desart bright,
Let thy moon arise,
While I close my eyes.

Sleeping Lyca lay;
While the beasts of prey,
Come from caverns deep,
Viewed the maid asleep

The kingly lion stood
And the virgin view'd.
Then he gambold round
O'er the hallowd ground

35

Leopards, tygers play,
Round her as she lay;
While the lion old,
Bow'd his mane of gold,

And her bosom lick,
And upon her neck,
From his eyes of flame,
Ruby tears there came;

While the lioness,
Loos'd her slender dress,
And naked they convey'd
To caves the sleeping maid.

The Little Girl Found

All the night in woe,
Lyca's parents go:
Over vallies deep,
While the desarts weep.

Tired and woe-begone,
Hoarse with making moan,
Arm in arm seven days,
They trac'd the desart ways.

Seven nights they sleep,
Among shadows deep,
And dream they see their child
Starv'd in desart wild.

Pale thro' pathless ways
The fancied image strays,

Famish'd

36

Famish'd, weeping, weak
With hollow piteous shriek

Rising from unrest,
The trembling woman prest
With feet of weary woe.
She could no further go.

In his arms he bore
Her arm'd with sorrow sore
Till before their way,
A couching lion lay.

Turning back was vain,
Soon his heavy mane
Bore them to the ground
Then he stalk'd around

Smelling to his prey,
But their fears allay
When he licks their hands
And silent by them stands

They look upon his eyes
Fill'd with deep surprise
And wondering behold
A spirit arm'd in gold.

On his head a crown
On his shoulders down
Flow'd his golden hair,
Gone was all their care.

Follow me he said,
Weep not for the maid;
In my palace deep
Lyca lies asleep.

Then they followed,
Where the vision led:
And saw their sleeping child,
Among tygers wild.

To this day they dwell
In a lonely dell
Nor fear the wolvish howl
Nor the lions growl

37

THE Chimney Sweeper

A little black thing among the snow:
Crying weep, weep, in notes of woe!
Where are thy father & mother? say?
They are both gone up to the church to pray.

Because I was happy upon the heath,
And smil'd among the winters snow:
They clothed me in the clothes of death
And taught me to sing the notes of woe

And because I am happy, & dance & sing,
They think they have done me no injury:
And are gone to praise God & his Priest & King,
Who make up a heaven of our misery.

NURSES Song

When the voices of children are heard on the green
And whisperings are in the dale:
The days of my youth rise fresh in my mind,
My face turns green and pale.

Then come home my children, the sun is gone down
And the dews of night arise
Your spring & your day are wasted in play
And your winter and night in disguise.

The SICK ROSE

O Rose thou art sick.
The invisible worm.
That flies in the night
In the howling storm:

Has found out thy bed
Of crimson joy:
And his dark secret love
Does thy life destroy.

THE FLY

Little Fly
Thy summers play,
My thoughtless hand
Has brush'd away.

If thought is life
And strength & breath.
And the want;
Of thought is death;

Am not I
A fly like thee?
Or art not thou
A man like me.

Then am I,
A happy fly,
If I live,
Or if I die.

For I dance
And drink & sing:
Till some blind hand
Shall brush my wing.

The Angel

I Dreamt a Dream! what can it mean?
And that I was a maiden Queen:
Guarded by an Angel mild:
Witless woe, was neer beguild!

And I wept both night and day
And he wip'd my tears away
And I wept both day and night
And hid from him my hearts delight

So he took his wings and fled:
Then the morn blush'd rosy red:
I dried my tears & armd my fears,
With ten thousand shields and spears.

Soon my Angel came again:
I was arm'd, he came in vain:
For the time of youth was fled
And grey hairs were on my head

The Tyger.

Tyger Tyger, burning bright,
In the forests of the night:
What immortal hand or eye,
Could frame thy fearful symmetry?

In what distant deeps or skies,
Burnt the fire of thine eyes!
On what wings dare he aspire?
What the hand, dare seize the fire?

And what shoulder, & what art,
Could twist the sinews of thy heart?
And when thy heart began to beat,
What dread hand? & what dread feet?

What the hammer? what the chain,
In what furnace was thy brain?
What the anvil? what dread grasp,
Dare its deadly terrors clasp?

When the stars threw down their spears
And watered heaven with their tears:
Did he smile his work to see?
Did he who made the Lamb make thee?

Tyger Tyger burning bright,
In the forests of the night:
What immortal hand or eye,
Dare frame thy fearful symmetry?

43

My Pretty ROSE TREE

A flower was offerd to me:
Such a flower as May never bore.
But I said I've a Pretty Rose-tree.
And I passed the sweet flower oer.

Then I went to my Pretty Rose-tree:
To tend her by day and by night.
But my Rose turnd away with jealousy:
And her thorns were my only delight.

AH! SUN FLOWER

Ah Sun-flower! weary of time,
Who countest the steps of the Sun:
Seeking after that sweet golden clime
Where the travellers journey is done.

Where the Youth pined away with desire,
And the pale Virgin shrouded in snow:
Arise from their graves and aspire
Where my Sun-flower wishes to go.

THE LILLY

The modest Rose puts forth a thorn:
The humble Sheep. a threatning horn:
While the Lilly white, shall in Love delight,
Nor a thorn nor a threat stain her beauty
                                    bright.

44

The GARDEN of LOVE

I went to the Garden of Love.
And saw what I never had seen:
A Chapel was built in the midst,
Where I used to play on the green.

And the gates of this Chapel were shut,
And Thou shalt not. writ over the door:
So I turnd to the Garden of Love.
That so many sweet flowers bore.

And I saw it was filled with graves.
And tomb-stones where flowers should be
And Priests in black gowns, were walking their
      rounds,
And binding with briars my joys & desires.

The Little Vagabond

Dear Mother, dear Mother, the Church is cold.
But the Ale-house is healthy & pleasant & warm:
Besides I can tell where I am used well,
Such usage in heaven will never do well.

But if at the Church they would give us some Ale,
And a pleasant fire, our souls to regale;
We'd sing and we'd pray all the live-long day;
Nor ever once wish from the Church to stray.

Then the Parson might preach & drink & sing,
And we'd be as happy as birds in the spring:
And modest dame Lurch, who is always at Church,
Would not have bandy children nor fasting nor birch.

And God like a father rejoicing to see,
His children as pleasant and happy as he;
Would have no more quarrel with the Devil or the Barrel
But kiss him & give him both drink and apparel.

45

LONDON

I wander thro' each charter'd street,
Near where the charter'd Thames does flow
And mark in every face I meet
Marks of weakness, marks of woe.

In every cry of every Man,
In every Infants cry of fear,
In every voice: in every ban,
The mind-forg'd manacles I hear

How the Chimney-sweepers cry
Every blackning Church appalls,
And the hapless Soldiers sigh
Runs in blood down Palace walls

But most thro' midnight streets I hear
How the youthful Harlots curse
Blasts the new born Infants tear
And blights with plagues the Marriage hearse

47

The Human Abstract.

Pity would be no more.
If we did not make somebody Poor:
And Mercy no more could be.
If all were as happy as we:

And mutual fear brings peace:
Till the selfish loves increase.
Then Cruelty knits a snare.
And spreads his baits with care.

He sits down with holy fears.
And waters the ground with tears:
Then Humility takes its root
Underneath his foot.

Soon spreads the dismal shade
Of Mystery over his head
And the Caterpiller and Fly.
Feed on the Mystery

And it bears the fruit of Deceit.
Ruddy and sweet to eat:
And the Raven his nest has made
In its thickest shade

The Gods of the earth and sea.
Sought thro Nature to find this Tree
But their search was all in vain:
There grows one in the Human Brain

INFANT SORROW.

My mother groand! my father wept.
into the dangerous world I leapt:
Helpless, naked, piping loud:
Like a fiend hid in a cloud.

Struggling in my fathers hands:
Striving against my swadling bands:
Bound and weary I thought best
To sulk upon my mothers breast.

A POISON TREE.

I was angry with my friend;
I told my wrath, my wrath did end.
I was angry with my foe:
I told it not, my wrath did grow.

And I waterd it in fears,
Night & morning with my tears:
And I sunned it with smiles,
And with soft deceitful wiles.

And it grew both day and night,
Till it bore an apple bright.
And my foe beheld it shine,
And he knew that it was mine,

And into my garden stole.
When the night had veild the pole;
In the morning glad I see;
My foe outstretchd beneath the tree.

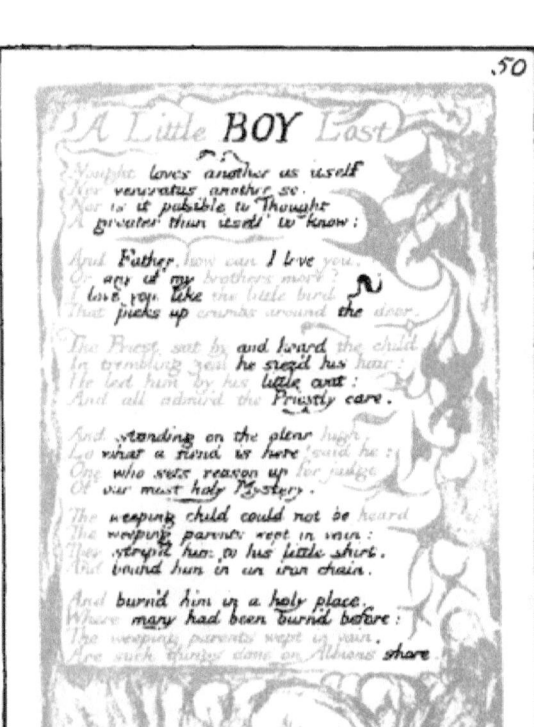

50

A Little **BOY** Lost

Nought loves another as itself
Nor venerates another so.
Nor is it possible to Thought
A greater than itself to know:

And Father, how can I love you,
Or any of my brothers more?
I love you like the little bird
That picks up crumbs around the door.

The Priest sat by and heard the child.
In trembling zeal he siezd his hair:
He led him by his little coat:
And all admir'd the Priestly care.

And standing on the altar high,
Lo what a fiend is here said he:
One who sets reason up for judge
Of our most holy Mystery.

The weeping child could not be heard
The weeping parents wept in vain:
They strip'd him to his little shirt.
And bound him in an iron chain.

And burn'd him in a holy place.
Where many had been burn'd before:
The weeping parents wept in vain.
Are such things done on Albions shore.

51

A Little GIRL Lost

Children of the future Age,
Reading this indignant page;
Know that in a former time,
Love! sweet Love! was thought a crime.

In the Age of Gold,
Free from winters cold;
Youth and maiden bright,
To the holy light,
Naked in the sunny beams delight.

Once a youthful pair
Fill'd with softest care
Met in garden bright,
Where the holy light,
Had just remov'd the curtains of the night.

There in rising day,
On the grass they play:
Parents were afar:
Strangers come not near:
And the maiden soon forgot her fear.

Tired with kisses sweet
They agree to meet,
When the silent sleep
Waves o'er heavens deep:
And the weary tired wanderers weep.

To her father white
Came the maiden bright:
But his loving look,
Like the holy book,
All her tender limbs with terror shook.

Ona! pale and weak!
To thy father speak:
O the trembling fear!
O the dismal care!
That shakes the blossoms of my hoary

52

To Tirzah

Whate'er is Born of Mortal Birth.
Must be consumed with the Earth
To rise from Generation free;
Then what have I to do with thee?

The Sexes sprung from Shame & Pride
Blow'd in the morn; in evening died
But Mercy changd Death into Sleep;
The Sexes rose to work & weep.

Thou Mother of my Mortal part.
With cruelty didst mould my Heart.
And with false self-decieving tears.
Didst bind my Nostrils Eyes & Ears

Didst close my Tongue in senseless clay
And me to Mortal Life betray:
The Death of Jesus set me free.
Then what have I to do with thee?

It is Raised a Spiritual Body

53

The School Boy

I love to rise in a summer morn,
When the birds sing on every tree;
The distant huntsman winds his horn,
And the sky-lark sings with me.
O! what sweet company

But to go to school in a summer morn,
O! it drives all joy away,
Under a cruel eye outworn,
The little ones spend the day,
In sighing and dismay.

Ah! then at times I drooping sit,
And spend many an anxious hour,
Nor in my book can I take delight,
Nor sit in learnings bower,
Worn thro' with the dreary shower

How can the bird that is born for joy,
Sit in a cage and sing,
How can a child when fears annoy,
But droop his tender wing,
And forget his youthful spring.

O! father & mother, if buds are nip'd,
And blossoms blown away,
And if the tender plants are strip'd
Of their joy in the springing day,
By sorrow and cares dismay.

How shall the summer arise in joy,
Or the summer fruits appear,
Or how shall we gather what griefs destroy
Or bless the mellowing year,
When the blasts of winter appear.

54

The Voice of the
Ancient Bard.

Youth of delight come hither.
And see the opening morn.
Image of truth new born.
Doubt is fled & clouds of reason.
Dark disputes & artful teazing.
Folly is an endless maze.
Tangled roots perplex her ways.
How many have fallen there!
They stumble all night over bones of the dead;
And feel they know not what but care.
And wish to lead others when they should be led.

www.ingramcontent.com/pod-product-compliance
Lightning Source LLC
Chambersburg PA
CBHW020409030726
47496CB00007B/2385